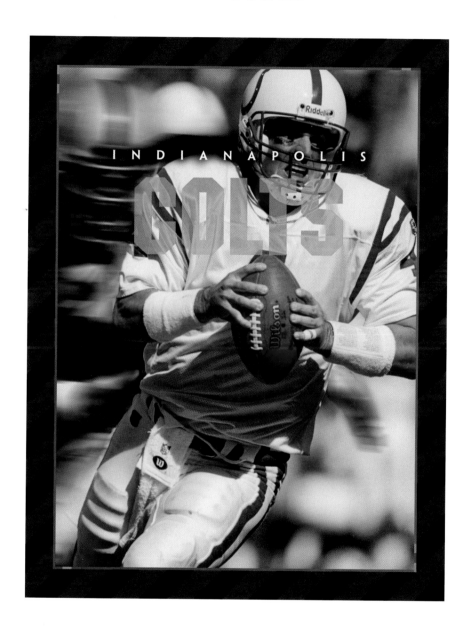

INDIANAPOLIS COLTS

LOREN STANLEY

CREATIVE EDUCATION

Published by Creative Education
123 South Broad Street, Mankato, Minnesota 56001
Creative Education is an imprint of The Creative Company

Designed by Rita Marshall
Cover illustration by Rob Day

Photos by: Allsport Photography, Associated Press, Bettmann Archive,
Focus on Sports, Fotosport, FPG International, and SportsChrome.

Library of Congress Cataloging-in-Publication Data

Stanley, Loren, 1951-
Indianapolis Colts / by Loren Stanley.
p. cm. — (NFL Today)
Summary: Traces the history of the team from its beginnings through 1996.
ISBN 0-88682-816-3

1. Indianapolis Colts (Football team)—History—Juvenile literature.
[1. Indianapolis Colts (Football team) 2. Football—History.]
I. Title. II. Series.

GV956.I53S83 1996   96-15238
796.332'64'0977252—dc20

123456

When the city of Indianapolis is mentioned, many people think of the Indianapolis 500, perhaps the most famous auto race in the world. But there's more to Indianapolis than the Indy 500. The city has more than 700,000 citizens and is the largest in the state of Indiana.

Located right in the middle of the state, Indianapolis is a city that has grown from a village of 8,000 people in 1850 to the fourteenth largest city in the United States. As Indianapolis has grown, so has the city's love of sports. Since 1984, Indianapolis has been home to one of the most loved teams in the National Football League—the Indianapolis Colts.

Johnny Unitas (#19) emerged as a great quarterback in the 1950s.

Most cities, when they get a new NFL team, have to settle for an expansion franchise that has no history and no established stars. The Indianapolis fans, by contrast, got an existing team with one of the richest traditions in the NFL. Robert Irsay, owner of the Colts, decided in 1984 that his franchise would be better in Indianapolis than in Baltimore, where the team had been for thirty years.

1 9 5 3

Defensive end Gino Marchetti joined the Colts after a superb career at the University of San Francisco.

So in the spring of 1984, moving vans appeared one evening in front of the Colts' office in Baltimore. The team's belongings were loaded into the vans, and the club moved to Indianapolis. The team brought with it three world championships and a heritage that included some of the greatest players in football history. Its home was now Indianapolis, but the team was still called the Colts.

UNITAS BRINGS CHAMPIONSHIP SUCCESS

T he Baltimore Colts played their first season in 1953. The team was formed out of what had been the Dallas Texans in 1952. The Texans were bad, so bad that they won only one game in 1952. But owner Carroll Rosenbloom made some very wise decisions, and the Colts started to improve.

First, Rosenbloom hired Weeb Ewbank as coach for the 1954 season. Under Ewbank, the team won more games every year. Then, before the 1956 season, the Colts gave a tryout to a young quarterback.

Who was Johnny Unitas? He was a man the lowly Steelers had decided wasn't good enough to be one of their three quarterbacks. But the tryout was successful, and the Colts put Unitas on the roster. In the fourth game of the 1956 season, starting

Jeff George was the quarterback in the early 1990s (page 7).

Already a legend— Johnny Unitas passed for 2,550 yards and twenty-four touchdowns during the season.

quarterback George Shaw broke his leg. Unitas was now the man in charge. The Colts finished 5-7 in 1956, and Unitas established himself as a star. In 1958, the Colts won the Western Division title and earned the right to play the New York Giants in the NFL championship game. The Colts were heavy underdogs, but Unitas and his teammates didn't care. The Colts were a young team, and they believed they could beat anybody.

Baltimore quickly raced to a 14-3 lead, but the Giants rallied with two touchdowns and were ahead 17-14 with just under two minutes remaining. Unitas and the Colts offense trotted onto the field. The ball was on the Colts 14-yard line, and nobody except the Colts and Johnny Unitas believed Baltimore had a chance. As the New York fans prepared to celebrate a championship, Unitas went to work.

Immediately Unitas completed a pass to Lenny Moore for 11 yards. Then he zeroed in on his favorite target, receiver Raymond Berry. A completion to Berry for 25 yards put the Colts at midfield. Unitas passed to Berry again, and the Colts were on the New York 34-yard line. Berry connected once more, and the ball was on the 13-yard line. With less than ten seconds left, Ewbank sent in Steve Myhra to try to tie the game with a 20-yard field goal. Myhra's kick split the uprights. The score was 17-17. For the first time in NFL history, there would be sudden-death overtime in a championship game. The first team to score would win.

The Giants got the kickoff in overtime, but couldn't move the ball and punted to Baltimore. The Colts started from their own 20-yard line. Unitas used the running of fullback Alan Ameche and passes to Moore and Berry to move the Colts down the field. With the ball at the New York 7-yard line, Unitas gambled and threw to Berry, who caught it for a five-yard gain. After the game, reporters asked Unitas why he risked throwing an interception when the Colts were in sure field-goal range. "When you know what you're doing," Unitas said, "you don't throw interceptions."

On the next play, Ameche blasted into the end zone for a touchdown. The Colts won 23-17. They were world champions, and Johnny Unitas, the quarterback who wasn't good enough to make the Pittsburgh Steelers, was the toast of the football world.

Lenny Moore scored twenty-four points for the Colts in a contest with Chicago.

In 1959, the Colts won their second consecutive NFL title, beating the Giants again in the championship game, this time by a score of 31-16. Unitas was being called one of the greatest quarterbacks ever to play the game. He had ability and a strong arm, but what separated him from other quarterbacks was his courage.

"You can't intimidate him," said Los Angeles Rams defensive tackle Merlin Olsen. "He waits until the last possible second to release the ball, even if it means he's going to take a good lick. When he sees us coming, he knows it's going to hurt and we know it's going to hurt. But he just stands there and takes it. No other quarterback has such class."

Behind the strength of his pinpoint passing, Unitas led the Colts to winning season after winning season—albeit no championships—in the 1960s. In the meantime he continued to earn the respect and admiration of teammates and opponents alike.

"People talk about how brave Joe Namath is, and that's true, but he's no braver than John Unitas. No one is," stated Colts linebacker Mike Curtis. "John has broken about every rib in his body, and he has suffered jammed fingers and a broken

The sure-handed Floyd Turner (pages 10-11).

nose and a broken elbow. Once he broke a rib and punctured his lung, and he had to have a tube inserted to drain the fluid from his lung. He played two weeks later."

Unitas had plenty of offensive weapons to use. Lenny Moore could run with the ball or catch it. Raymond Berry may have had the best hands of any receiver in the game. In addition, the Colts had a powerful tight end, John Mackey, who could run over tacklers once he caught the ball.

On defense, the Colts had such stars as Billy Ray Smith and linebackers Don Shinnick and Dennis Gaubatz. During the 1960s, new coach Don Shula built one of the best stopping forces in football. One of the key members of that defense was a man they called "The Animal" or "Mad Dog." The Colts fans would never forget Mike Curtis, no matter what they called him.

12

Mike Curtis didn't care if you called him "The Animal" or "Mad Dog." He just wanted you to know that, off the field, he was an intelligent person. But on the field, Curtis knew his job was to destroy offenses anyway he could.

Curtis was drafted by the Colts from Duke University in 1965. He soon became a starter for Baltimore as an outside linebacker. He also got a reputation as a very hard hitter. "We were playing Green Bay," said Baltimore linebacker Ted Hendricks. "Jim Grabowski was coming through the line, and Mike Curtis gave him a good old-fashioned clothesline shot. He hit him so hard it popped his [Grabowski's] helmet off. Grabowski got up wobbly. One of our guys handed him his helmet. He started heading for our bench. I tapped him on the shoulder and turned him around and said, 'Yours is on the other side, Jim.'"

With Curtis wreaking defensive havoc on the field, the Colts were again a dominant team. They won the NFL title in 1968, with Earl Morrall replacing the injured Unitas at quarterback. But the Colts lost 16-7 in the Super Bowl to the upstart New York Jets and Joe Namath. Two years later, the Colts were in the Super Bowl again, this time against the Dallas Cowboys. Unitas, who had led the team there, got hurt in the second quarter and was replaced by Morrall.

The Colts, who trailed 13-6 at halftime, tied the game in the fourth quarter. Then it was Mike Curtis's turn to be a hero. With less than two minutes remaining, Dallas quarterback Craig Morton tried to move his team for the winning score, but Curtis had other ideas. Morton rolled out to the right and threw downfield; the ball was tipped, and Curtis ripped it out of the air.

1 9 6 0

Super streak snapped! Johnny Unitas completed touchdown passes in an NFL-record forty-seven straight games.

13

Bubba Smith was an All-Pro for the second consecutive season.

He returned it to the Dallas 28-yard line. Three plays later Jim O'Brien kicked the game-winning field goal, and the Colts won 16-13. They had claimed their third world championship.

In 1971, the Colts believed they had an even better team. Curtis, who had moved to middle linebacker, was the key man in a nasty Baltimore defense that also included huge defensive lineman Bubba Smith, linebacker Ray May, and safeties Rick Volk and Jerry Logan. The Colts, who were now playing in the Eastern Division of the American Football Conference, didn't win their division in 1971. (The American Football League and the National Football League merged in 1970. The Colts were one of the three teams shifted to the new American Football Conference from the NFL.) The Colts did, however, make the playoffs. But Miami, coached by former Colts head man Don Shula, defeated Baltimore 21-0. Miami advanced to the Super Bowl, while the Colts headed home.

As the 1972 season began, the Colts faced a rebuilding project. The team had gotten old. In addition, the Colts had a new owner. Carroll Rosenbloom had owned the Colts since 1953, but in 1972, Rosenbloom actually traded the Colts for the Los Angeles Rams, a franchise that had just been bought by Robert Irsay. Irsay was the Colts' new owner. The team also had a new general manager; Joe Thomas, who had engineered the trade of the Rams and the Colts.

One of Thomas' first moves was to trade Unitas to San Diego after the 1972 season. Johnny Unitas' reign in Baltimore had ended. When he left Baltimore, he held NFL records for most pass attempts, most pass completions, most yards passing, and most touchdown passes. To this day, even though almost all of his records have been broken, Unitas is still considered one of the top quarterbacks in NFL history.

14

Bert Jones spearheaded the Colts' passing attack in the 1970s.

The Colts finished 5-9 in 1972, and the fans in Baltimore blamed Thomas for the team's sudden decline. When Thomas traded Unitas, the fans wanted the general manager's scalp. But Thomas was more interested in finding a new quarterback.

1 9 7 3

Ted Hendricks, a future Hall of Famer, made his third Pro Bowl appearance.

JONES JAZZES UP THE COLTS

Thomas knew who he wanted: Louisiana State University quarterback Bert Jones, who had been around pro football all his life. Jones' father, Dub, played and coached with the Cleveland Browns during the 1950s and 1960s. "I grew up around the Browns," Bert Jones remembered. "When I was in high school, I was ballboy for four years at their camp."

Jones was the Colts' first-round draft pick in 1973. The young quarterback spent most of his time on the bench as Baltimore posted records of 4-10 in 1973 and 2-12 in 1974. Thomas knew the team needed a change, so he hired an offensive-minded coach, Ted Marchibroda. It was the best thing that could have happened as far as Jones was concerned. Marchibroda was a former quarterback who knew the position as well as anyone.

"Ted did a mental job on me," Jones said. "We studied films, playbooks, theory, the whole thing. We even graded the other clubs we'd be playing and figured how we might attack them."

When the 1975 season began, Jones was the Colts' starter. Baltimore won its first game, but then lost four in a row. In the next game, the Colts trailed the New York Jets 21-0 at halftime. Baltimore fans screamed for a new quarterback, but Marchibroda was determined to stick with Jones. His decision paid off: Jones and the Colts scored six touchdowns in the second half and won 45-28. The Colts just kept on winning. In

Lenny Moore struggles to recover the football.

Eric Dickerson had the first 100-plus game of his record-breaking career.

the final two games of the regular season, Jones engineered comeback victories over Miami and New England. The Colts, who had started the season with a 1-4 record, won nine in a row to finish 10-4 and claim the team's first division title in five years. Although Baltimore lost to Pittsburgh 28-10 in the first round of the playoffs, the future looked very bright. In addition to Jones, the Colts had stars in running back Lydell Mitchell and tight end Raymond Chester.

Despite all their talent, the Colts struggled during the 1976 preseason, losing four of six games. Owner Robert Irsay fired Marchibroda, but Jones wouldn't stand for that. Jones told Irsay that if Marchibroda wasn't rehired, Jones would leave the team at the end of the 1976 season. Irsay rehired Marchibroda.

Jones' leadership inspired respect from his teammates. Before a game in 1976 against the Houston Oilers, Jones had

a bad case of the flu. But he played anyway, and he led the Colts to victory. "He was so sick yesterday that I thought he'd fall down if an Oiler so much as breathed on him," said offensive lineman George Kunz the next day. "But he played another great game. He's heady, he's tough, he's wild. It kind of rubs off on the rest of us."

Together, Jones and the Colts took care of winning. They won the AFC East in 1976 and 1977, but lost in the first round of the playoffs both times. But the winning ways didn't last. Mitchell was traded to San Diego in 1978, and Jones started having trouble with injuries. Marchibroda was fired after the 1979 season. The Colts had risen to the top very quickly under Jones; unfortunately, they fell just as quickly to the bottom. Once last place became a reality, the Colts decided to build for the future, so they traded Jones to the Los Angeles Rams in 1981.

Chris Hinton's talent shined in his fifth Pro Bowl appearance.

The "Baltimore" Colts never had another winning season. After the team went 7-9 in 1983, Irsay decided he had had enough of Baltimore. A group from Indianapolis talked Irsay into moving the team to that city. It wasn't a tough sell. Indianapolis had just finished building the 60,000-seat Hoosier Dome, a beautiful indoor stadium.

The Colts had a new home, but they were still losers. Frank Kush, a defensive-minded coach, was replaced by Rod Dowhower. But the team didn't have enough talent to compete. In 1986 Indianapolis lost its first 13 games. General manager Jim Irsay, son of the owner, fired Dowhower and named Ron Meyer as the new coach. Meyer had an immediate impact, and the Colts won their last three games of 1986. Suddenly, hopes were high for 1987.

Fredd Young (#56) came to Indianapolis via the Seattle Seahawks.

DICKERSON RUNS TO INDIANAPOLIS

The Colts were an improved team in 1987, but Irsay found a way to make the team much better with just one player. He wasn't just any player, though. He was the best running back in the NFL.

No runner had as quick a rise to the top as Eric Dickerson. Drafted by the Los Angeles Rams in 1983, Dickerson led the NFL in rushing his rookie year. He was the main weapon in the Rams' offense—sometimes he was the only weapon. By 1987, though, Dickerson no longer wanted to play for Los Angeles. He felt he should be paid more, but the Rams refused to rewrite his contract. Finally, Dickerson told the Rams to trade him.

The trade was finally made in early November 1987. When Dickerson joined the Colts, Meyer already had the team believing it could win. Running back Albert Bentley was a solid runner and pass catcher, and receiver Bill Brooks was a deep threat. But the best part of the Colts offense was the line: center Ray Donaldson, guard Ron Solt, and tackle Chris Hinton were all Pro Bowl players. Dickerson and Bentley both had success running behind this trio. On defense, linebacker Duane Bickett led the team in sacks and was also a Pro Bowl pick.

All of this talent combined to lead the Colts to a 9-6 record in 1987, which was good enough to win the AFC Eastern Division title. The Colts had made it to the playoffs for the first time in ten years, but they lost in the first round to Cleveland 38-21. However, it was obvious that the Colts had become contenders.

In 1988, Indianapolis made two key additions. The team obtained linebacker Fredd Young in a trade with the Seattle Seahawks and drafted a quarterback, Chris Chandler, who had

1 9 8 9

Colts center Ray Donaldson made his final Pro Bowl appearance.

Left to right: Bill Brooks, Chris Hinton, Rohn Stark, Eric Dickerson.

an immediate impact as a rookie. Chandler beat out veteran Jack Trudeau for the job and led the team to a 9-7 record. Unfortunately, that wasn't good enough to qualify for postseason play. The following year, injuries sidelined Chandler for almost all of the season and Dickerson for part of it. Trudeau filled in for Chandler, but he couldn't lead the hurting Colts to the playoffs.

During the 1990 NFL Draft the Colts traded Hinton and wide receiver Andre Rison, as well as draft choices, to the Atlanta Falcons for the number one pick in the draft. The Colts then selected University of Illinois quarterback Jeff George and signed him to a $15 million contract.

1 9 9 0

In his rookie year, quarterback Jeff George accounted for 2,152 passing yards.

George enjoyed a solid rookie season in 1990, throwing 16 touchdown passes. But the veteran Dickerson was now on the downside of his career, and the Colts lacked a solid running game to balance the offense. Further, the aging defense unit was weak both against the pass and the run. The Colts finished 7-9 that year and then plummeted to 1-15 in 1991.

It was time to rebuild—starting with a new head coach. Ted Marchibroda, who had made the Colts winners in Baltimore in the mid-1970s, was hired again in 1992 to do the same in Indianapolis. In the NFL Draft that spring, the Colts had the top two picks—and Marchibroda bolstered the Colts defense by selecting defensive tackle Steve Emtman and linebacker Quentin Coryatt.

In training camp, Marchibroda set a standard of dedication that quietly inspired his players. Coaching, he believed, was "a 24-hour-a-day job. No motivating speech is going to make the difference. You have to work with your football team every minute to get it ready to play on Sunday."

Lamont Warren takes on Charger defenders (pages 26-27).

1 9 9 6

Ellis Johnson was a first round draft choice with impact on the club.

Marchibroda's leadership paid off. With a record of 9-7, the 1992 Colts tied the all-time NFL mark for best turnaround in a single NFL season—posting eight more wins than the previous year. But the team slumped the next season, and George was traded to the Atlanta Falcons. Marchibroda knew that he needed immediate help both at running back and at quarterback.

The first need was taken care of when the Colts made San Diego State running back Marshall Faulk their number one pick in the 1994 NFL Draft. Faulk wasted no time in proving that he could make the jump to the pro ranks, rushing for more than 100 yards in his first two games. He went on to become the NFL Offensive Rookie of the Year.

Clearly, the Colts had found their running back. But filling the quarterback position wasn't as easy. Jim Harbaugh, who had spent seven years with the Chicago Bears, was signed as a free agent in 1994. But Harbaugh didn't have a good year, and Craig Erickson—obtained in a trade with Tampa Bay—was penciled in as the starter for the 1995 season. Harbaugh, it was decided, would serve as his back-up.

But it didn't work out that way. Harbaugh rebounded with a "career year" in 1995, passing for 17 touchdowns and leading Indianapolis to a 9-7 record and a Wild Card playoff berth. Then the "Cinderella Colts"—as they were dubbed by the national media—startled the experts by upsetting the defending AFC champion San Diego Chargers 35-20 in the first round and the powerful Kansas City Chiefs 10-7 in the second round. After that contest, Chiefs tackle Will Wolford paid tribute to the Colts quarterback: "Forrest Gump should be as fortunate as Jim Harbaugh. He's been magic this year."

The following week, in a memorable AFC championship game, the Colts were narrowly edged by the Pittsburgh Steelers 20-16. The outcome came down to the final play, when Harbaugh

Sean Dawkins refuses to be tackled.

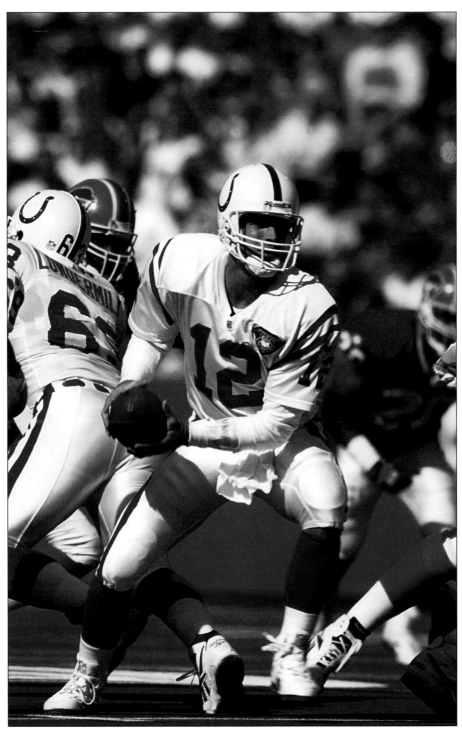

Quarterback Jim Harbaugh proved that he could lead the Colts.

Marshall Faulk broke through to running stardom in the 1990s.   31

Jay Lewenburg's skills bolster the Colts' offensive line.

lofted a "Hail Mary" pass from the Pittsburgh 29-yard line into the right corner of the end zone. Despite the frantic efforts of the Steelers defense to bat away the football, Colts receiver Aaron Bailey almost came up with it as he fell to the ground. Instead, the ball bounced off his hip—and Pittsburgh held on for the hard-fought win.

Still, the Colts could hold their heads high. No longer a "Cinderella" team, they had emerged as a proven AFC contender. After the 1995 season, Colts offensive coordinator Lindy Infante was named as the new head coach to continue the team's winning ways. Indianapolis fans now have high hopes for the 1990s. They remember the Colts' past glory days in Baltimore, and they are ready for a new championship era of their own.